nick jr.™

W9-AXV-397

Sunny Day™

Country Style!

Adapted by **Tex Huntley**

Based on the screenplay **"Sunny's Not-So-Simple Concert"** by Jodi Reynolds

Illustrated by **Miranda Yeo**

A Random House PICTUREBACK® Book

Random House 🏠 New York

rhcbooks.com
ISBN 978-0-525-64849-9
MANUFACTURED IN CHINA
10 9 8 7 6 5 4 3 2

Glitter effect and production: Red Bird Publishing Ltd., U.K.

Sunny, Rox, and Blair had spent a busy morning buying supplies for the salon. They felt they had earned an ice cream break.

"Let's see," Rox said, looking at the selections. "Strawberry Swirl, Chocolate Cheesecake, or Banana Berry? It's so hard to choose."

Just then, Sunny heard a beautiful voice singing a song.

Sunny followed the sound and spotted . . . Johnny-Ray with his guitar!

"I was just playing a little tune for Suzette," he said, patting his horse.

"You could be a country star!" Sunny exclaimed. "We should put on a show—tonight!"

"Okay, Sunny," said Johnny-Ray. "If you say I should do a show, I'll do a show—as long as it's small, simple, and low-key."

"Absolutely," Sunny agreed.

Back at the salon, Sunny and her friends started preparing.
"What better way to spread the word about a country-music
concert than with some country hairstyles?" Sunny suggested.
Sunny, Rox, and Blair braided their hair with pieces of
gingham, and Doodle put on a bandana bow tie.

While Johnny-Ray practiced at the salon, Sunny and her friends went into town to tell everybody about the show. They met Cindy outside her bakery and discovered that she knew how to play the spoons! Sunny asked her to perform at the show.

"You can be his backup spoons!" Sunny said.

She also asked Peter to help. He could make music by rubbing some vases from his flower shop.

Sunny and her friends went to the park to check on the concert stage. They found it crowded with ballet dancers.

"It looks like the ballerinas are practicing for their next recital," Rox observed.

"I'll ask them to be Johnny-Ray's backup dancers!" Sunny exclaimed.

When Johnny-Ray arrived at the park, Sunny whisked him into the Glam Van for a country-star makeover.

"I just need my Number Four comb, some super-stick hairspray, and glitter," said Sunny.

"Glitter?" Johnny-Ray asked.

Before he knew it, Sunny had given him a whole new look. Rox, Blair, and even Suzette barely recognized Johnny-Ray.

A little while later, Blair gave Sunny a status report.

"The lasers are set up on the stage," she said, "and the ballerinas are practicing their do-si-dos."

It was time for the final sound check.

"For that, we need Johnny-Ray," said Sunny.

But he was nowhere to be found.

"Why would Johnny-Ray leave?" Sunny asked her friends. "This will be the biggest and best show ever!"

That was when Sunny remembered that Johnny-Ray had wanted a small, simple show.

"I didn't listen," she said. "Now I have to make this right."

Luckily, Doodle could speak Horse. He told Sunny that Suzette knew where to find Johnny-Ray. Sunny hopped in the Glam Van and followed the galloping horse across town.

Johnny-Ray was sitting sadly in his wagon by the boardwalk.
"I'm sorry," Sunny told him. "I broke my number-one rule:
always listen to what the customer wants."
"It's okay," Johnny-Ray said. "You were only trying to help."
"Will you give me a chance to fix this?" Sunny asked.
"Okay, sure!" said Johnny-Ray.

First, Sunny had to get the real Johnny-Ray back.

"I need to give you a makeover . . . in reverse," she said.

After a few moments, Johnny-Ray looked like himself again.

Suzette whinnied her approval and put his cowboy hat on his head.

Johnny-Ray felt good. "It's showtime!" he declared.

Unfortunately, with so many people heading to the concert, there was a lot of traffic.

"It looks like we'll never get there in time," Johnny-Ray said sadly.

"Never say never!" Sunny exclaimed. She and Johnny-Ray jumped onto Suzette and galloped between the cars.

Suzette reached the park just in time, and Johnny-Ray hopped onstage with his guitar.

"This first song is for my good friend Sunny," he announced.

Sunny smiled as Johnny-Ray started to sing. The crowd went wild. It was a small, simple, and low-key show . . . and it was really, really fun!